SHE'S MY POETIC
PHILOSOPHY

SHE'S

MY

POETIC

Philosophy

TECOLA SMITH

Mind Finesse

MIND FINESSE LTD

Published by Mind Finesse Ltd, London, UK

"To the challenges in life"

I dedicate this book to truth.

We can only see and know our own versions of reality; our reality is
created through our own experiences.
Our perceptions of the world around us are unique.

Tecolasx

Acknowledgments

I would like to say thank you to Lo Designz an amazing young black female designer who created this amazing book cover. I also want to thank my mother who always believed in me, even when I didn't believe in myself, she would remind me and encourage me to continue.

Thank you to all the experiences that have inspired me over the years, I appreciate you and I am very grateful for your contributions to my life

Table of Contents

What's your poetic philosophy?

INTRODUCTION

Have you ever met someone that just believes in you without reason? an individual that surprises you with support and acknowledgement at a time in your life when you just couldn't see it for yourself. That person for me was Miss G my Year 10 and 11 secondary school top set girl's English teacher. I never thought that writing was something that a person could be talented at, in my 14-year-old mind everyone could write. I started expressing myself through short stories around the age of 7 years old, I would read the dictionary and thesaurus daily so that I could use big words in my stories to impress my mom and anyone that wanted to listen. By the time I was 14 writing poetry was a daily routine and I began to trust Miss G so I opened up about my poetry and would read them to her in some of my dinner breaks. Miss G was so timid, she had very fair hair, which was extremely thin for her age, she used to hunch over when she walked and was extremely shy and reserved. She always spoke so negatively about herself, but she loved her job and had a passion for teaching and believing in her students which was something I was not used to receiving from a secondary school teacher. By year 11 we had developed a good teacher/student relationship and I felt comfortable with sharing my most expressive words with her. She told me that one day I would be an author. At that time, I did not see what she saw in me, I did not realise that the one thing in my life that I could do so effortlessly with passion could be a career, so I laughed it off and said, ok. Miss G suffered from mental health issues and near the end of year 11 left abruptly and I never saw or heard from her again. I am now 32 years old, and this is my first self-published book, I finally realised that this is my true passion, this is my saving Grace and the power in words are real and healing and she is my poetic philosophy, Thank you Miss G.

I wanted to create a book of real emotions with poetic language, versions of someone else's reality but using my words. I wanted to contribute to the acceptance and overcoming of life struggles, an attempt to explore HER the woman in all of us. She is a very important concept and represents the birth of all thoughts and all versions of our life for me. These poems have been written from years of listening, observing and living, the beauty of poetry is storytelling and that there are no rights or wrong ways to express and create through words. The acceptance of fluidity and adaptation in the way that life presents itself. The lines from my reality entering into yours can be blurred, which is why I hope that you read without judgement, I want you to read each poem like you wrote it, understand each poem in the way you want to understand it, allow it to resonate with whatever feelings you have of it. These poems are about 'She' and she has no name, she could be all of us, she might be you, she is already Me. Join me and divulge into these poetic stories of truth, life, realism, heartache, pain, resilience, self-love, empowerment and much more.

Life is my inspiration, how hard some days are, then in a flash how encouraging and great other days can be. I have worked over the years in many different industries and witnessed the struggles, the wins that surprise you through those struggles and much more. Through all the poems I have felt, I believed, and I developed which is all I could ask for. This chapbook is no ordinary poetic book, let's say it is a chapbook with a twist. My intentions are to inspire your voice, so you can be part of this experience. Use this chapbook as your tool to capture your words, tell us your poetic philosophy, document what you feel. Many of us can relate to the many rollercoasters of life. While you read through this collection of poems, acknowledge your emotions, and engage in these feelings, there is a surprise at the back for you. Life has taught me great lessons and gifted me with a level of resilience to a world that is undeniably shifting. My appreciation I cannot express enough, I just hope that I have been able to reinvent these experiences, to hopefully educate, inspire and relate to anyone that takes the time to read this book of poetry. Even though these are an amalgamation of the experiences of many people, I believe they each reflect a time in a person's life that is relatable and demonstrates that we are not alone in our feelings and thoughts. She is all of us with a voice that needs to be heard. This is a poetic journal a safe place to discuss the adversity and strength of the female and our lives.

#SHEISPOETIC

Social not just Media

The Social side of her media,
has more effect on her perception of her exterior,
masses being created in this generation of mental enslavement,
confused by this arrangement,
to wake to flick through pages,
the need for this consistent engagement,
Breeds the epidemic we're facing,

No likes affecting your reality,
Unrealistic embedded in this tragedy,
You believed you didn't give a f*ck,
But the f*ck is why you gave in when no one was hitting you up,
So you delete,
but you can't delete the hurt you feel the most creeping in your sleep
Captivated but in reality, you feel like a ghost in defeat.

Invisible, the most beautiful queen,
Got her blinkers on while she's glaring at her screen,
but still, she feels the need to conform to the posting
Snapchat, snaps the chat because you chose to snap back doing the
most
soliciting your body due to boredom,

No decorum
Mental health is soaring.

She's anxious because she's anxious about the anxiety that she feels.
But you remain in the remains of the anxiety loop because you're
anxious about the unreal.

"Even after the ferocity of a storm, Beauty makes it self-known."

Media Minds

The Master mind behind the masters of our minds ain't us,
She put it into people she doesn't know,
but seems to trust.

If you read between the lines it cries out it's so apparent,
the system is a master mind our institutional parents.

Like a child groomed to not know true adversity,
to never understand the meaning of our life's version of university.

Depression on life lessons, our youth lacking resilience
Delirious individuals, evolution isn't quick enough,
Systems moving quicker than our humanitarian development
Scared, but this generation ain't ready for this intelligence.

No longer separated, by what was beyond our communities
She see's the flossing of all and still lacking opportunities.

So much vanity that she can't afford, her result is to sell, snort and
extort
She doesn't feel education is her passion, it isn't her escapism.

She sees so many build empires to inspire but forget where they
came from.

She laughs, thinking it's all a game, but if you don't play it right, you'll be mind f*cked with no one else to blame.

"We find ourselves always trying to seek acceptance as if anything we do requires an applause from the masses and without the cheers and fans singing our praises it can't be considered as enough or even good enough. We are in a time where people create a persona for the world to see because unless your life is extraordinary, it's not ordinary, we portray this as who we are until we actually forget who we are. The question you should be asking yourself is who am I and from that honesty your true quest can begin."

#SHEISPOETIC

ONLY IF

Spoken out of turn she feels destroyed, she lost her composure,
he slid in her DMs, banged, then got over her.

So insecure, she does the only thing she knows,
gets back on da gram, looking for someone else to blow.

Lord knows, the true pain that she's feeling,
but she hides behind the smile,
so, you only see her grinning.

Pretty selfies, looking ever so perfect,
but perfection isn't pertinent,
when you're feeling so imperfect.

Stumbling through life,
she's no longer a teen,
but the back alleys and hotel rooms was the only love she's seen.

No, this isn't a dream.
it's the life that she's living,
so many thoughts she's had with her hanging from her ceiling.

It's true pain that she's feeling
Remembering her reason,

Why she ended up on this path

From that one moment

She was lit and left bleeding.

"Through the MIST of all things CLARITY is still a POSSIBILITY"

Boredom #Idle

Done with the flicking, life feeling so mediocre
drawn to analyse herself, she starts feeling like a joker.

Bored now a little depressed, she starts feeling manic
her life to her is shit, so it's got her in a panic.

She starts stressing,
cortisol pumping through your veins,
it's so depressing.

You don't realise the more you increase your levels,
the more you feel insane,
so many thoughts now piercing through her brain,
it's no game.

The pressure is building up,
so, her only relief is to release, so she chooses to cut
Ahhhhhh she breathes out with a sigh,
'feelings' so emotional,
whaling out with a cry,

Your temporary relief wasn't a release so now you in a state,
why is life so hard, why ain't it on a plate.

Question?

Only if she knew how to count her blessings.

She has a family, friends but still, she's here overly stressing.

"Forgiveness can take a day, but Resentment can take a life and time."

My Dear Diary

Dear diary, I'm domesticated but not dominated, sophisticated is what I am. It's got nothing to do with the fact I can sing, IVE GOT A MAN.
Boss and Bad, don't call me a Bitch.
My moves are in silence, never played a loud game, my monopoly is outstanding it's a capitalisation mind game.

Point me out I am my husband's wife, but I'll be damned to be called nothing but a housewife.
I have houses don't get me twisted, I move bricks without the motor, my foundation is set stronger than the cake on my face, your puff won't falter.

Act like you know nothing and say even less, never let me down,
Sitting at the table never the clown,
 I watch and clock, lock in and block all the sly shade,
You will never knock my crown,
it will always be my mind game.

#SHEISPOETIC

"Make your mind explore the world in which we live, encourage your soul to be spiritually unbound, refuse to be obscure by the relentlessness of your passions, guide your flesh through to overcome the physicality of your environment, connect your being to supremacy of that it can be and is."

Too Friendly

Genuinely, I laugh at the notion, HA!
my circle maybe small but don't be fooled
all witches brew their potion.

Too much mixed emotions
fearing to talk up,
find it quick to walk up.

To collect, when it's their token.
I move differently, I've never been blind,
My eyes beaming open.

I don't care me; I've got mine and it's 3
all I need is them and they always got me.

Girls are laughable,
Men stay half full, or is it empty?
Depending on the side of the table,
please don't tempt me.

I will never be suppressed or blinded by the caress against my
breast,
I'm not here to impress.
You can indulge!!!
But beware cuz if you lie too much, my dogs will bite the end of that
nose.

Don't move to slow, you need to speed up,
the rat race will have you broke not peed up.
So be mindful who you stand with,
the devil has no bounds on who he crosses lines with.

Their energy stays foul, like the shit you don't speak,
but spoke loud with that fake smile and kiss on my right cheek.

Like I said girls are laughable,

Men half empty or is it full?
Either way, I played my move
And now I'm done with the bull.

"I sit calm, centred at peace, aware, present and accepting. I embrace my thoughts as they are and let them pass through me with ease and without regret, I shall and will not dwell on misfortune and the inability to control all things."

I AM CALM

Who's system

It's not my fault I live the life I live,
poverty stricken since I was a kid.

It's not my fault my father was not around, it's his fault I became the
whore of my town.

It's not my fault I failed at school,
the teachers hated me which made me act like a fool.

It's not my fault I got pregnant with this kid,
it's my baby fathers' fault I'm unemployed living like my mom did.

It's not my fault I have this life,
all the successful people had it handing to them,
"I know I'm right".

You don't understand the struggles I've been through,
cuz nobody else in the world has it hard like I do.

I blame the government always trying to hold me down,
only the rich and famous have it easy in my town.
I know I ain't to blame that my life is a shame,
it's not my fault, everyone else is to blame.

It's not my fault, I'm only a kid

if it is my fault, this isn't the life that I'd live.

I'm too used to blaming everyone else for all the things that I DID.

"We are either moving forward or moving backwards, time is a continuum that does not allow us to be still."

Not *A product of her environment*

Sitting in the doctor's office, can't keep her food down.

She's already very thin weighing so few pounds.

"Please lord" she's begging don't be what I think.

She runs to the toilet vomit in the sink.

So many plans, I start uni in a month.

I can't deny this change in me or this little bump.

My mom is a church sister, I'm a Pastors Kid.

Running to the toilet vomit in the sink.

Can I be forgiven; can I just repent?

What's that verse in the bible, remind me of what Jesus said?

Abortion is my testimony; I need this, can I ask!

My family will only disown me no matter what my path.

#SHEISPOETIC

"Your original step never actually moves you forward, it's the step that follows."

Mentally Drowning

Clouded with no room to even think.

The pressure of the pounding is so hard,

she just closes her eyes, so she can't even blink.

Darkness behind the emptiness that she feels,

overcome by her mental drowning of the secrets she's so scared to

reveal.

Warm with a hint of salt

trickles like a stream,

but the background noise is so loud,

it pushes her to the extreme,

there's no silence in this dream,

or is it her reality,

is it as it seems?

Her mind is like the hell she created,

captivated without any words left to speak,

"It's so cold in here"

she opens her eyes; the tears fall with only one blink.

Alone with no one to care,

but she's sat in a room full of her friends

sitting with only a stare.

In her eyes no transparency,

illusions with no clarity.

She hides her demons well and so deep

suffocating her mentally,

slowly drowning until she sleeps.

Why did I trust in him?

Why didn't I think?

The scrub like a scour

shooting razors across her skin.

Loose enough to fold, not hold my mouth, it was covered I tried to scream,

no sound just like a ghost, pinned down in my dream.

If only I could say or pray to release that demons grin.

Now I am a Sin.

Where do I begin?

"If you remained as fascinated as a child is experiencing the taste of a new food or as determined as a baby taking his or her first steps, how amazing could your life feel."

Colourism by a Colourist

Brown not black,

am I chocolate? that's a fact.

Salted caramel am I your flavour or is a lighter shade what you

favour.

Darkness is spreading yeh laugh out loud,

the clown of the crowd.

I know you still see me,

acting like you can't hear me.

I will be the center of your joke,

don't laugh to hard, you might hopefully choke.

I'm an artist I work with all shades of brown,

the darkest shade to the lightest I'm down.

You ain't to partial,

 you say our tones can't catch,

but it's funny how me and your mothers colour is a direct match.

You think I am your enemy

because in your neighbourhood my dark skin draws in a lot of

negative energy.

Sisters with many shades

is what we are.

Our race ain't changing so we are what we are.

Black, Brown, Lighty they say even if it's only an ounce,

You really think the KKK would hesitate to pounce

Only we clocking our Shadism like we don't already have to deal

with socioeconomic racism

"Meditation keeps me sane, but writing keeps me inspired"

Her Voice

"I'm drowning", I'm in that place

can you relate?

It's something I'm struggling daily to face.

I can't concur my demons,

they are trying to destroy me.

I fall to my knees,

hoping that the feeling stops controlling me.

Gets erased,

the first time in my life, I felt this disgrace.

That I was.

Unclear, unclean, broken, truly destroyed,

but there was a voice that rang clear through the back noise,

it spoke out so anointed,

"I love you child don't feel so disappointed. Come out the corner the

suffering is over,

it's your time to climb on my back, so I can lift you on my shoulder,

I will carry you from here, just pace yourself, cause this ride won't

be easy. It's an easy way out, as long as you open your heart, faith

and allow me to guide you freely,

so, you can see the women you are through your own eyes, no

you're not dreaming, let down your disguise."

She sits up released of her burden,

no longer feeling drawn to the external yearning.

Proud and beautiful, feeling so clean,

walking smiling wide,

knowing she's a queen,

released from the hurt child she has always been.

"Circumstances happen and I say it like that because it is only a moment in time, if I formulate a sentence around the word, I am giving it life, so yes circumstances are moments, but it's the aftermath of that moment which can feel like a lifetime. In actual fact, that is the only part that you can control, how you choose to handle the aftermath of a circumstance is a choice, so it is up to you and in your control, inevitable yes uncontrollable no."

She Speaks Out

"I asked the question?
I'm in this paradox of this obsession,
"I can see now I do have some blessing"
But the controversy of my mind
tries to keep me guessing,
I fall back daily pulling myself through,
I have so many questions now, it would turn your face blue,
"So many things that I believed to be true"
Was it only my creation controlling everything I thought I knew?
I'm seeing things I didn't see, but I'm exposed to the same things
that was always in front of me,
I wasn't blind but I could not see
the visions of my own prophecy,
The things that made me, Me.
She is still, centred, focused and ready,
No longer in contemplation, or consumed by the bullshit on the
Telly,
Frequencies amplified no static in her belly,
But her, she flies no one can keep her steady.
No more, slow mo, in her motions, the cocooned life prepared her to
be freed from these emotions.

"We take food for granted until we run out of food.

We take family for granted until death knocks at their door.

We take our health for granted until we are diagnosed with a terminal illness.

So, let's not take time for granted, we have a limited supply, but with that supply we can choose what we do where and with whom we choose to spend it."

My Friend Rose

Born to a society already against me

Bred into this world designed to hate me

You sense it, but can't always see it

Have you thinking it's you and got you believing it?

You leave your soul at home and walk naked on the streets

She doesn't really condone, but a kid needs her sweets, and I don't
mean candy.

She sunk quicker than a sand pit covered in water,

People looking knowing she's somebody's daughter.

This fallen angel, why did she fall out of heaven

This fallen angel, why did you fall out of

heaven

To this birth,

Did I ask to be on this earth?

Crying sounds eerie, echoes against the baseline rhythm

Her heart now pounding, what has she taken

White dust, felt like a must, to get into her feelings,

But when her cash flow was low, it had her climbing the ceilings.

Now her hearts racing, she's overly pacing,

thinking how high she wants to fly.

So, she hits the street, it's the only way she knows how to get bye.

This fallen angel, why did she fall out of heaven

This fallen angel, why did you fall out of
heaven
To this birth,
Did I ask to be on this earth?

She comes home, well to the room that she's living in.
She feels numb, as a result of the injecting
thoughts so poisonous.
Depressing and Stressing.
So much more than this label,
she climbs on her last bed, but it's actually a table.
She takes a step forward to make it unstable.
She shivers and it ain't a result of the cold,
she's so out of this world she doesn't realise the final breathe fall
from her nose.
This time it's not a dream her eyes closed shut
that's the last thing our angel seen,
never to wake up.

This fallen angel, why did she fall out of heaven
This fallen angel, why did you fall out of
heaven
To this birth,
Did I ask to be on this earth?

Her room is now a crime scene,
people in the block can't believe what they have seen.

Her roommate found her hanging,

how can this happen, her grades were outstanding?

Who would have thought, being at university?

she's meant to have some sort of mental stability,

but the pressure of the studies and student community,

was more than she could handle,

It just wasn't meant to be, her life was in a mangle.

She chose the roads to escape the pressures of the lifestyle her
family chose,

until that pressure killed their only daughter, and her name was
ROSE x

This fallen angel, why did she fall out of heaven

This fallen angel, why did you fall out of
heaven

To this birth,

Did I ask to be on this earth?

"Through the Mist of all things CLARITY is still a Possibility"

A Lost Soul

Breathe, air colder than the sea breeze.

Rain feels the frills of flash backs in her daydreams,

seeing it as I see you, not knowing what the f*ck to do.

Breathe, the shudder and Bang,

so close range, ain't it strange that it wasn't stranger. Lay in waiting

as he lay waiting, your presence now gone. What went wrong?

Breathe, in his breath was depth then death,

senses sense the distress as I digress.

I fall to sleep in these cold wet sheets unable to catch my breath.

The moment he could no longer…

Breathe, sharp and staggered,

slower and lower, loss of power

the engine can't turn over,

slower and slower, my game is over

It's getting harder to breathe.

Breath, distress, scared to rest,

In case I forget to breathe,

Are my days over, fingers crossed, and toes numb?

It's getting colder and colder,

no sense, can sense the change

no longer in pain,

Today I don't want to breathe.

Waking up in a sweat,

chest pounding, is it over yet.

His night stare is my nightmare.

The darkness and silence in those moments no solace.

When you stole his last chance to breathe.

"To understand her life, you must understand time and the lack of restraint around what we define and constrict our minds to associate time and timing with. The power of difference and the perception of difference. Time is a continuum so cannot be subjective, which is why time is perfect in the essence of what it truly represents and that is ABSOLUTELY NOTHING."

Locked Down

It's 3am, I can't sleep again,
this lockdown has my mind racing
insomnia here again.

Home life is hard I'm struggling to keep up,
my 9 to 5, Master's Degree and 3 kids have me consumed and still
my eyes can't shut.

Exhausted by fatigue, SLE leave me please.
I try stay motivated constantly feeling guilt my daughter feels I
don't get it.
But I do, I'm so conflicted with my day job and studying sometimes
I do forget about playing with you.

Nursery runs every day no energy left,
no health benefit to this lifestyle I set.
In play, but still by the end of the day
my mind is racing, pacing about the things I'm not doing,
thinking should I change the things I'm pursuing.

Lockdown has me locked down why did I allow it?
That's a question I asked myself everyday but still I'm bound by it.
My own personal prison pushed by my mind's decision, to section
me in the sections that I find it hard to sleep.
My meditation is affected when I try my best to deep breathe.
I need to relax, I'm confined by these four walls, boxed in by the
boxes I perceive.

I have to escape, before I lose myself to this pandemic misplace.
As I sit in this now horribly familiar place, every day I say the same
thing. When will this all be over?
I guess in my mind is where that will begin.

#SHEISPOETIC

44

"To the readers even if it is just one reader, stop measuring your progress against someone else's time because time is infinite and is only representable to the time capsule you choose to measure it against. Treat it as the infinite energy that it is and work within whatever frame of time that suits you and your lifestyle best."

Still Born

Your heart cries for an angel so precious,
Emotional but hormonal digresses your truthful expressions.
Be not that she may, you bare such to lay
Believe the belief, for the beauty could not stay,
All has happened within reason,
Such things create disorientation and confusion.
Your strength surpasses all expectation,
Refusal to let experience cloud your determination.
She bares the pain, so deep, in this it shall keep,
Lay dormant sweet fear, nor shall seek.
For as small and ever so significant
The life began to beat.
But such life is a beauty,
No matter how long, your heart did beat.
He called out and home you went,
So fruitfully blessed, in the short time you spent.
You were touched for the first time with a child's unconditional love
and Beauty,
The time was not in vain, she completed her duty.
You now know love like no other,
As you may have heard,
There is no love like the love of a Mother.

"In darkness even the smallest trinket of light

is at its brightest"

The woman in the Mirror

Overcome with resentment, blurred but visibly clear,

The woman in the mirror, who is she?

Full it's black, so dark in here, she shivers, presumptuous could this be,

The woman in the mirror, who is she?

Encapsulated by this disillusionment, is this to be,

The woman in the mirror, who is she?

No more, no one, two or three, I refuse this to be,

The woman in the mirror, who is she?

Mind is full, now so mindful, this knowledge is free,

The woman in the mirror, who is she?

Freedom to think, so freely, she can be freed,

Finally, the woman in the mirror, I can see, that she is me.

'She stood so tall that all fell mellow beneath her feet'

She's Beautiful

She seeks beauty outside of herself,

She cries aloud expecting all else to help,

She feels alone within a crowded space,

She shouts out, but dwells in pure heart ache,

She acts, it's her new persona,

She is discouraged because nobody knows her,

She smiles but bleeds in seas of sorrow,

She laughs it echoes through empty hollows,

She's beautiful more than she knows,

She has so much to offer her aura glows,

She has these eyes so deep and full,

All she needs is a friend to pull her through.

#SHEISPOETIC

"Act as if you do, then do as you then begin to act".

Emotional Health

I'm feeling overwhelmed, unsatisfied, why?

I'm happy, in love, why?

I hate my job, why?

I love my career, why?

I read, I write, why?

I smash things, I cry, why?

I'm so unsure, why?

I'm so sure, why?

Pain, so painful, why?

Happiness, so happy, why?

I'm angry, frustrated, it's all frustrating, why?

Emotionally unstable, physically bound, mentally free and spiritually alive, I'm living and I don't care why.

'Your Action will always be louder than the whispers of Dialogue'

#Graduation meltdown

Went, I studied hard for the years it stole my mental capacity.

Modules by the many, practical competencies.

Deciphering remits to accomplish a classification that labels me.

No other room for more than my covered shades could see.

Mental Emptiness because they set me free.

Structures formed around the structured living.

Compliancy created from my routine beginning.

Let loose, left for the wolves to devour.

I thought education was meant to empower.

3 years of my life now only is my life beginning.

Fear itself can never know this feeling.

So unsure, but graduation means I'm leaving.

So, I threw my hat and smiled as a graduate.

There're no bounds now to what I can be achieving.

So, I stopped, exhaled, and just kept believing.

'Escape solitude to gain affinity'

Ungrateful Child

Overlooked so graciously, my importance not yet so clear,

to those who inhabit me continuously insincere.

I oppose with my wrath, soaring through with seas of tears,

I crash and smash but still only a few here, hears.

Like a parent I provide unconditionally with no judgements,

stripped back, stripped bare without any consequence.

Eyes cannot see, but bodies will feel,

as my existence starts to quiver.

Neither I nor they shall heal,

As our existence begins to disappear.

Breathe so deep, electronic connections we share,

Abuse will kill all and leave all in despair.

I mean no harm, but harm is all I endure,

Progressively aggressive until all is war.

Breathe so sweet my children as time is so dear,

Breathe sweet my children as you continue the end shall one day be here.

'At the root of desire lay dormant pain and despair'

Me vs You

Your my silent enemy moving so slow inside of me,

creating pain, fatigue and messing with my biology,

inflammation all over riddled with your aggression,

many days of cries stressing, this is my confession,

a moment so beautiful you tried to take it from me,

cutting my oxygen, raising hell so I couldn't see,

blasting and smashing my organs,

your fine attempt of art,

you would never of guessed 22 year old me had such strength in my heart,

your attempt to kill me,

but I was to strong, my beautiful baby girl growing made me determined to live on,

so tiny born to soon,

but between you and my enemy I'm glad it took the spare room,

you was safe in my arms, that's all that mattered,

I had the cuts and scares but still I wasn't shattered,

9 years later, full of health,

until they found two heart beats, there was concerns for my health,

but I already knew, I had it sussed,

no enemy before me can win in higher power I knew I could trust,

you came on time and surprised them all,

I was given the strength and I built a strong wall,

to block you from danger and myself,

but the moment you both was removed so was my good health,

but that's ok,

I stay thankful every day,

I was blessed with you three,

my big daughter and twins you was a gift to me,

so let me tell you SLE,

you maybe my silent enemy, but no matter what I now understand,

I have the power and my life is in my beautiful three.

#livingwithlupus

"There is no need to fear regression it is a true realisation that regression only indicates that you have progressed and experienced growth, as you can't regress from nothing. Rather than fearing regression embrace it, learn from it, recreate it and start again."

"There will always be a beginning. There will always be an end. 'But the stuff in between could be amazing"

I WILL SEE YOU ALL AGAIN SOON

Explore, Be Creative & Enjoy

WHAT'S YOUR POETIC PHILOSOPHY?

Write with your heart not with your mind

This Book Belongs to

_____

THE END

Made in the USA
Coppell, TX
21 August 2021